20,000 Leagues Under the Sea

By Jules Verne

A new version of the
classic tale of adventure
by Archie Oliver

HINKLER
BOOKS

Cover Illustration: Terry Riley, sga Illustration & Design, Hadleigh, Suffolk, UK
Illustrations: Mike Lacey, sga Illustration & Design, Hadleigh, Suffolk, UK
Editor: Heather Hammonds
Typesetting: Midland Typesetters, Maryborough, VIC, Australia

 20,000 Leagues Under the Sea
This adaptation published in 2004 by
Hinkler Books Pty Ltd
17–23 Redwood Drive
Dingley VIC 3172 Australia
www.hinklerbooks.com

© Hinkler Books Pty Ltd 2004

ISBN 1 7412 1023 2
Printed and bound in Australia

The Author
Jules Verne (1828–1905)

Jules Verne was one of the most popular writers of his time and has sometimes been called the father of science fiction.

Born in Nantes, France, Verne's father was a lawyer and his mother came from a family of ship builders, and seafarers. He was fascinated with travel from an early age and even tried to run away to sea when he was twelve. He studied law in Paris as a young man, but he soon gave up his studies to concentrate on his first love – writing.

The author of more than one hundred exciting novels, plays and short stories, Verne accurately predicted many future scientific inventions and events, such as submarines, guided missiles and space travel. He keenly studied the scientific discoveries of the time and wrote about them in many of his books.

Other successful novels by Verne included *From the Earth to the Moon*, *Journey to the Center of the Earth* and *Around the World in 80 Days*, to name just a few.

Contents

1	Monster of the Deep	1
2	The Beast Sighted	7
3	The Chase	13
4	Inside the Monster	20
5	Captain Nemo	26
6	The *Nautilus*	33
7	An Incredible Voyage Begins	41
8	A Stroll on the Ocean Floor	48
9	Grounded!	54
10	Ashore	61
11	The Coral Cemetery	67
12	The Giant Pearl	75
13	The Tunnel	84
14	Volcano!	91
15	The Captain's Treasure	99
16	Visit to the Lost Continent	108
17	Southbound	115
18	The South Pole	123
19	Trapped Beneath the Ice	129
20	The Giant Squid	136
21	The Captain's Diary	144
22	Under Attack!	150
23	Murder and Maelstrom	158
24	The Captain's True Identity	167

Glossary

You will find these words in the book:

frigate	a type of fast warship, used by the navy
hull	the outer body of a ship, usually made of steel or wood
icebreaker	a strong ship with a special thick hull, used for breaking through ice at sea
league	an old measure of distance; the equivalent of three miles or five kilometers
maelstrom	a powerful sea whirlpool
man-of-war	any warship used by the navy
nautilus	a sea creature enclosed in a spiral shell
sextant	a special instrument used for finding a ship's position when it is at sea

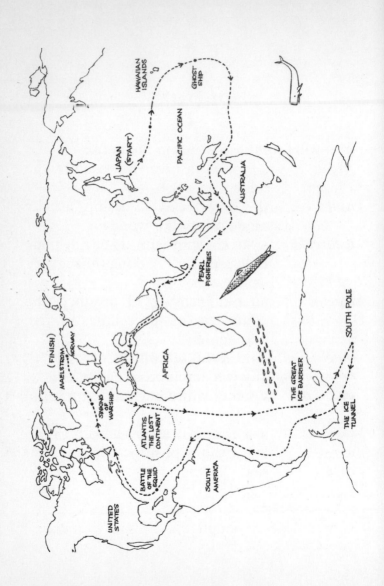

Chapter 1
Monster of the Deep

On April 14, 1866 the headline of the *Times* newspaper in London cried out:

Sea monster attacks English warship in Pacific Ocean!

A week later, the New York newspapers reported that a large passenger ship steaming across the Atlantic Ocean towards England had been rammed from below by a mysterious creature.

A few days afterwards, there were reports from the Indian Ocean that an "enormous thing" had collided with another European warship.

The hulls of all the ships involved in these incidents were holed below the water line. Fortunately, all managed to limp to port safely. But what extraordinary creature was the cause of these events? What monster could have sliced its way through the English warship's two-inch steel hull?

The year of 1866 was marked by several very strange and unexplained sightings of this mysterious beast, haunting the world's oceans. No one had actually got a good view of the creature. Some said it was a long, spindly-shaped thing, but much bigger than the biggest whale. It had been spotted on every ocean.

What astonished everyone was the monster's speed. One day it might be seen in the Pacific Ocean, the next in the Atlantic and the day after that in the Indian Ocean.

It was the talk of the most senior scientists in New York, Paris and London.

Newspapers called for a search of the oceans to hunt down the beast, before it sank a ship. They offered a large reward for anyone who captured it.

It was later announced in New York that a major scientific search expedition was to be mounted the following year. It would be led by Captain Farragut aboard the frigate, *Abraham Lincoln*.

I was asked to join the expedition. My name is Monsieur Pierre Aronnax, and I am a professor at the Museum of Natural History in Paris. The reason I was asked was because I had written several books on the world's oceans.

What was the cause of these events?

The excitement of the coming voyage was intense. What would we find? What was this monster of the deep?

I traveled to New York and went aboard the *Abraham Lincoln,* accompanied by Conseil, my servant of many years. As Conseil always said, "Wherever Monsieur goes, I go too."

The *Abraham Lincoln*, which was well prepared to kill or catch the beast, put to sea immediately. Aboard the ship were fixed guns with barbed harpoons and several other large weapons, capable of firing a nine pound shell several miles.

And better still, on board was Ned Land, a French Canadian from Quebec. A tall man, with a strong arm and keen eye, he was renowned as the world's finest harpooner of whales.

We headed south, rounding Cape Horn at the tip of South America and sailing into the Pacific Ocean on July 6, 1867. By July 20, we were in the area where the monster had last been sighted.

The *Abraham Lincoln* criss-crossed the Pacific Ocean for the next three months. We found nothing. On the evening of November 5, the decision was taken to return home. The sea was calm, the water rippling peacefully beneath

Aboard the Abraham Lincoln

made no difference. The monster was still moving towards us at twice our speed.

We gasped for breath. Amazement, rather than fear, left us speechless and motionless. This animal was not only gaining on us, but seemed to be playing with us as well.

It circled us a few times and then moved off, leaving a shining luminous trail behind it. We all thought it had gone, but it had only moved away to mount an even faster charge on our ship.

Out of the darkness it came, rushing at a terrible speed. We fell to our knees in prayer. It would cut us in half. Then just as it drew close, the light vanished beneath us, only to emerge on the other side of the ship a moment later.

"It must be a giant whale," called the captain.

"But an electric one too," I added.

As if to surprise us just one more time, the monster disappeared. The light we had seen beneath the surface vanished. That was followed by a deafening hiss, and roaring jets of water bursting from below.

"Ned," asked Captain Farragut, "have you ever heard a whale roar?"

"Indeed, sir, many a time" said Ned, "but I never ever saw a whale that glowed like this one."

"It's coming straight at us!"

"And those jets of water?" asked the captain.

"Whales do blow water from their vents," he replied. "But it would have to be a real monster whale to do what that creature has just done."

Soon after we saw the light again, but this time it was some miles away. We imagined we could hear the beast panting for breath, and the sound of its tail thrashing on the surface.

Night fell and we waited uneasily in the darkness.

The next morning we saw that the creature had not moved. But in daylight we had a clearer view of it. It had a long gleaming body, as if it were covered in large shiny scales. It wasn't completely on the surface and only part of it was visible, but its thrashing tail could be clearly seen.

For a moment, it looked as if it was powered by a propeller.

Captain Farragut now moved his ship closer in and I got a better view of the beast. It was about three hundred feet long and some thirty feet wide. As I watched, two jets of steam and water suddenly burst out from its vents. There was no doubting it now. This was a whale of some kind, but one of such size that it was almost beyond belief.

The Beast Sighted

The creature had not moved.

The captain prepared for attack. "Full steam ahead!" he ordered

A few minutes later, the *Abraham Lincoln*'s two funnels were throwing out clouds of black smoke. The deck shook with the vibrations of the engines at full power.

Ned took up his position by the main harpoon gun right at the front of the ship. His finger was on the trigger!

Chapter 3
The Chase

The creature waited until we were quite close and then raced off.

"More speed!" cried Ned.

What a chase! I was trembling with excitement. I gradually became aware that every time the ship increased speed, so did the creature that was racing beneath the waves in front of us. It never allowed the ship to get close enough for Ned to fire his harpoon.

The beast was playing with us again. At midday we were no closer than we had been at eight o'clock that morning.

"Right," said Captain Farragut, "if the thing can outrun us, let's see if it can beat a shell from our guns."

The master gunner loaded and fired. The shell flew just above the target.

"Someone with a better aim!" cried the captain. "Five hundred dollars to the man who can pierce the hide of that infernal beast!"

An old gray-bearded gunner stepped forward and loaded the next shell. He aimed slowly and deliberately, and fired. The shell hit the target, but something extraordinary happened. It simply bounced off the creature and sank harmlessly into the water.

"Confound the thing!" roared Captain Farragut. "I'll go after the beast until my ship blows up. The animal must tire eventually."

But despite an all day chase, the "thing" always stayed well ahead.

At dusk, the brilliant light we had seen the night before reappeared and the beast finally slowed down. At last it appeared to be motionless, as if sleeping after a hard day's work. Captain Farragut saw his chance. He ordered the ship to "Dead Slow." His plan was to creep up slowly on the beast.

The ship approached silently, until it was just two hundred yards away. The light from the creature was now absolutely dazzling. Closer, ever closer went the ship. I saw Ned ready, with his harpoon raised. On deck you could have heard a pin drop.

Suddenly, Ned's arm straightened and the harpoon shot out. I heard a deep ringing sound, as though it had struck a hard surface.

What a chase!

Immediately, the dazzling light went out and two enormous jets of water landed on the *Abraham Lincoln*'s decks. The water swept like a torrent from one end of the ship to the other, knocking men over by the dozen. I felt a blast and was flung over the ship's rail, and out into the sea.

When I recovered my senses, I was under the water. My first thought was to wonder if anyone aboard the *Abraham Lincoln* saw me

The harpoon shot out

go overboard. Would I be rescued?

By now it was almost dark. I looked around me but I could not see the ship at all.

My clothes had now become waterlogged. They were starting to pull me under. "Help! Help!" I shouted.

Suddenly, I was grasped by a firm hand and I heard the following words: "If Monsieur would lean on me, he might find it easier to swim."

With one hand, I seized the arm of my faithful Conseil. When I recovered my breath I asked if he had been thrown into the water too.

"Oh no, Monsieur," he replied. "I am always in Monsieur's service. When I saw you fall in, of course I had to follow."

"Where's our ship?" I asked before swallowing another mouthful of seawater.

"Gone," said Conseil. "The monster turned on us and smashed our rudder. The ship can no longer steer."

"Then we're lost," I said.

"Perhaps," said Conseil calmly. "But, Monsieur never knows. We could yet be saved."

The water had now chilled me to the bone. I was starting to slip away. Almost as if he was asking if I wanted a cup of tea, I heard Conseil say: "Does Monsieur require some help?"

"Where's our ship?"

I was too far gone. I slipped beneath the surface.

The next thing I knew, I felt something hard bumping into me, and then someone tugging at me. I was sure it was Conseil pulling me up again. But no. As I surfaced, the moon came out and I saw the familiar face of Ned, hauling in both myself and Conseil.

It turned out that Ned had also been thrown overboard. "I was luckier that you," he said. "I landed on the giant beast. It was like a floating island."

"You landed on the beast?" I gasped.

"Not so much of a beast in fact," said Ned. "Unless it's a monster made of steel. That's the reason our shell and my harpoon bounced off it. The beast we have been chasing is made of steel. Just look around you."

It was then that my eyes became dimly aware that we were now all clinging to the back of the creature we had chased for so long.

Chapter 4

Inside the Monster

There could be no doubt whatsoever. The animal, the monster, the beast that had intrigued experts from all over the world was made of steel. And the strangest thing of all was that I could hear haunting sounds of organ music coming from inside it.

By now I had forgotten all my worries about cold and fatigue. I wanted to know more. Here we were, clinging to a marine craft – a kind of underwater ship – which as far as I could judge, was the shape of a fish but made of steel. "There must be a crew inside it," I said.

"There must be," agreed Ned. "And yet, I've been aboard this floating island for three hours and seen no sign of life."

Just then, there was a bubbling sound behind us. It was a propeller starting to turn. The ship was moving again and we had to hang on tightly to prevent ourselves from being thrown into the water. Fortunately for us, it soon stopped.

Clinging to a marine craft

"Monsieur," said Conseil, "it is to be hoped that it doesn't dive."

It didn't dive, but sometime just before dawn it suddenly started to move again.

We would have all been thrown off except that Ned found an iron mooring ring which we all clung on to.

"A thousand devils," cried Ned. "Is there anyone inside? Open up, you monstrous creature!"

Then the strangest thing happened. The vessel did stop and there was a loud noise of bolts being pulled open from inside. A hatch opened onto a small platform above us, which was surrounded by iron railings. A man appeared and when he saw us, he uttered a strange cry and disappeared inside again.

A few moments later, eight more men appeared. Without uttering a sound, they dragged all three of us down into the machine. The hatch slammed shut behind us.

We were dragged down a narrow staircase, our feet occasionally touching the rungs of an iron ladder. When we reached the bottom I heard a door open. Then we were thrown inside a room. The door clanged shut and was bolted behind us.

We were alone in complete blackness.

We were dragged down a narrow staircase.

"Let us out of here!" Ned shouted angrily.

Suddenly, a light came on. Its dazzle blinded us for several minutes, but gradually we saw that we were imprisoned in a tiny cabin. I couldn't tell how long we were in that cabin. Ned was like a wild caged beast.

"Where are those pirates who are keeping us here?" he cried. "If they think they can keep me suffocating in this cage, they're very much mistaken."

Eventually the door opened and a member of the crew appeared. It was too much for Ned. Before I could make a move to stop him, he hurled himself at the man and caught him by the throat. The man was choking in Ned's powerful grasp.

Conseil and I were trying to drag Ned away when a large figure appeared in the doorway.

"Stop this at once," said a voice, with a perfect English accent. "Be good enough to stop this wrestling and listen to me."

The man spoke with such authority that Ned instantly released his prisoner. Tall and broad-shouldered, he wore a fur cap, sealskin boots and waterproof clothing. He had a darkish complexion, a strong straight nose and flashing white teeth.

He was without doubt the most remarkable man I had ever seen. There was something about his eyes that was most unusual. They seemed to bore into your very soul.

This was a man who clearly expected to be obeyed.

Chapter 5
Captain Nemo

The man examined us for a while before speaking again. "My intelligence tells me you have arrived here by chance," he said, "yet I must make it clear that you are intruders in my life."

"I insist that you free us at once," I said firmly.

"Free you!" he cried. "Your ship fired a shell at my vessel. You waged war on me. I think that makes you my enemy."

"We thought we were chasing a creature or an animal of some kind," I protested. "A civilized man would not call us an enemy just for making a mistake."

I will never forget what he said next. "I am not what you would call a civilized man. I have broken with society. I do not belong to your civilization any more, so I don't have to obey any of your so-called civilized laws."

There was anger in his eyes as he continued. "I could have left you on the deck of my ship to

"*I insist that you free us at once.*"

drown," he said. "At least you are still alive, even if you are now prisoners-of-war."

"This is against all international law," I replied.

"I will say it once more," he answered. "I do not belong to this world. I have my own laws. But since fate has brought you here you will have the freedom of the ship, apart from certain times when events may compel me to confine you to your cabins. I have no wish to use violence against you, but you must promise to obey my orders."

I asked the man how long he intended to keep us prisoner.

"Forever!" he said sharply. "You have stumbled on my secret. If you think I can send you back to your world with the knowledge of my existence, then you are mistaken. I am just protecting myself, my crew and my ship."

"Do we have a choice?" I asked.

"Yes," he replied. "Accept my offer or be thrown overboard, never to be seen again."

"A choice of life or death," I said.

"Exactly," he replied coldly.

This strange man then announced that he knew me.

"You may not know me, Professor Aronnax,"

he began, "but I know you and your work. Your books are in my library. I read them constantly. I know your interests, and I know that you will not regret your time as my prisoner. In the next few months you are going to travel through an underwater wonderland. I doubt you will ever stop being amazed and astonished at what you see. You will be my fellow student as we journey underwater around the world. And our planet, thanks to me, will deliver up to its last secrets."

The man's words had a powerful effect on me. For a moment I even forgot that the price

Master of the Nautilus.

of all this was my freedom. "And who am I addressing?" I asked at last.

"Captain Nemo," he said. "Master of the *Nautilus*."

The captain then told us to follow him. Outside our prison, we found ourselves in a long corridor. It was brilliantly lit, but not by gas. The astonishing thing was that it appeared to be lit by some sort of electricity. This was unheard of. This was the age of gas lights. No one had electric lights!

He turned into a large dining room. There was a meal on the table.

"You might not recognize some of the food," he said, "but you can eat everything without fear. All my food comes from the sea. The sea supplies all our needs on board, not just food. Our clothes are made from fibers grown on the ocean floor. My pen is made of whalebone. Ink comes from the squid."

"You talk of the sea as if it were a friend," I suggested.

"I do," he said, with a strange faraway expression on his face. "The sea is everything. It covers so much of the earth's surface. It is a vast reservoir of nature. It is my kingdom, and if you think me a tyrant, you are wrong. The sea

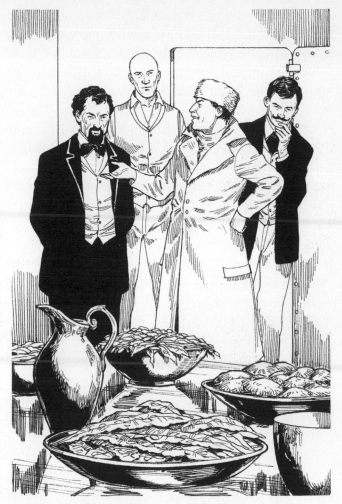

"All my food comes from the sea."

does not belong to tyrants. Thirty feet below the surface of the sea, tyrants cannot survive. Their world vanishes. No, below the surface we have perfect tranquility. Only here can freedom be found. Here I recognize no master. Here I am free!"

Suddenly, amidst this burst of enthusiasm, Captain Nemo became silent. Did he doubt what he had said? Was he just boasting? Another thought came to me, too. Was he mad?

For a few moments he walked up and down, obviously very agitated.

At last he gathered his thoughts together again. "Right, Professor," he said, "would you like to inspect the *Nautilus*? I am at your service."

Chapter 6
The Nautilus

Captain Nemo showed Conseil and Ned to their cabins at the rear of the ship, and then took me on a tour of his nautical castle.

He was very proud of the *Nautilus*. It was, he said, three hundred feet long and shaped like a long cylinder; almost cigar-shaped. It was thirty feet at it widest point, and had two hulls for extra strength.

The entire ship ran on electricity. That was extraordinary because most ships of the time were driven by coal. Electricity drove the *Nautilus'* engines, pumps, instruments and heating. The captain would not tell me how the electricity was produced. All he would say was that the secret lay in seawater and an electrical process.

Every room contained a duplicate set of the ship's main instruments. And each room had an electronic speaking link to the engine and steering areas. The captain could give orders to change the speed and direction of his vessel from anywhere on board.

Apart from the cabins, the first main room Captain Nemo showed me was a vast library. "There are twelve thousand books here," he said, "including yours, Professor."

Next door to the library was a magnificently decorated drawing room, some thirty feet long. All around the walls were paintings by such masters as Leonardo da Vinci, Raphael and Delacroix.

"They are souvenirs from a world that is dead for me now," he said. "They are worth millions in my old world, yet nothing beneath the waves."

In one corner of the room was a table, covered by a huge map of the world. The captain explained that the map was marked every few hours with the latest position of the *Nautilus.*

The main wall of the drawing room was shaped by the curve of the exterior hull. It was covered with steel panels on rollers. What did they hide? Captain Nemo wasn't ready to tell me yet.

Next door to the drawing room was something even more spectacular. It was a vast museum. I had never seen such a priceless

A magnificently decorated drawing room

collection of items taken from the oceans of the world. There was everything from specimens of long-vanished creatures to deep-sea ocean pearls the size of hens' eggs.

Next to the museum was Captain Nemo's cabin. The walls were hung with original paintings of George Washington and Abraham Lincoln.

In one corner there was a massive church organ. That was the source of the music I had heard from outside the ship. The instrument was covered with original musical scores by composers such as Mozart, Beethoven and Wagner.

"I am as dead as any of them," said the captain. "But hopefully I will leave behind a legacy as valuable as theirs."

My cabin was to be the one beside his.

After looking at the vast engine room, Captain Nemo gave orders for the *Nautilus* to surface. I heard pumps begin to empty the buoyancy tanks. In a very short while they stopped.

"We have arrived on the surface again," he said.

I followed him down the ship's main corridor. It was here that I saw a painting of a woman

36

hugging two children. I wondered if it was his wife and family. We reached the main staircase in the center of the ship. I recognized it from the ladder that I had stumbled down as we were captured.

"Open hatches!" called the captain.

Suddenly, daylight appeared from above, and we climbed onto the small platform that Ned, Conseil and I had seen before. It gave a view all around the ship. In front of the platform was a cage made of reinforced glass. This was where the helmsman steered and controlled the ship, both on the surface and below it.

Beside the platform was a large hatch. Captain Nemo explained that it led to a water-tight compartment with a dinghy inside. It could be launched on the surface or even at several hundred feet beneath the water, in an emergency.

"Well," said the captain, "what do you think of the ship?"

"I am astonished by everything I have seen," I replied. "Today we are only halfway through the nineteenth century. Yet I can imagine that the twentieth century will never see such a creation. The *Nautilus* is more than a hundred years ahead of her time!"

I had to ask him how such a ship had been built without anyone finding out.

"Each part of the ship came from a separate source," he said. "No one ever saw the whole picture. The keel came from France, the propellers from London, the engines from Germany and all the precision instruments from America. Each part was ordered under a separate name and sent by different routes to my secret island in the Pacific Ocean. There my *Nautilus* was built."

It frightened me that the captain was telling me so much. I realized with a chill that any hopes of my being freed decreased with each secret he told me.

"You must be a very wealthy man," I said at last.

"Very rich indeed, Professor," he answered with no emotion at all. "I am fabulously rich. I could pay off the national debt of France if I so chose."

I wondered where his staggering wealth came from.

Captain Nemo took out his sextant and took some navigational measurements.

"Today is November 8, 1867," he announced, after a while. "The time is midday. And we are

"What do you think of the ship?"

three hundred miles off the coast of Japan. Our voyage of exploration beneath the world's oceans is about to begin."

Chapter 7

An Incredible Voyage Begins

"Prepare to dive!" cried Captain Nemo, after we had returned below decks.

I left him and returned to the drawing room. Both Conseil and Ned were there.

"Where are we?" asked Ned, looking about. "Are we in a museum in Quebec?"

"Are we in a Paris art gallery?" asked Conseil.

"My friends," I replied, "we are not in Canada, nor in France. We are aboard the *Nautilus* and will soon be several hundred feet beneath the Pacific Ocean"

"If Monsieur says so," said Conseil, "then it must be."

I briefly told them about my talk with Captain Nemo and then asked what they had found out.

"Nothing," said Ned. "I have seen no crew, either. How many crew would it take to run a ship like this?"

I knew immediately what Ned was thinking.

He was wondering whether we might overpower them and take over the ship.

I warned him against the idea. "This ship is a masterpiece of technology, light years ahead of its time. Its captain is a ruthless man. I am sure he would not hesitate to throw us overboard if he felt we were endangering his mission . . . whatever that is."

Suddenly, the ship's pumps were heard. The angle of the ship changed – we were diving. All the drawing room lights went out and we were

"Where are we?"

left in total darkness. Then we heard something moving.

"What's going on?" cried Ned.

Two powerful lights at either end of the drawing room burst into life. To our astonishment, we saw that the panels of the hull wall had been drawn back to reveal a huge window. Never had I seen such a view! The sea was distinctly visible for almost a mile or more. We could see creatures of every kind, just inches away from our window.

"This is like being in an aquarium," said Conseil excitedly.

"Perhaps," said Ned. "The only difference is that we, not the fish, are the prisoners!"

That remark left me deep in thought. Who was the strange Captain Nemo? What nationality was he? Who or what had made him hate mankind?

The next morning there was no sign of Captain Nemo. But there was a note on our breakfast table.

It read:

To Professor Aronnax,
On board the Nautilus,
November 9, 1867.

Never had I seen such a view!

An Incredible Voyage Begins

Captain Nemo invites Professor Aronnax and his friends on an excursion to the forests of Crespo.

Signed:
Captain Nemo, Commander of the Nautilus.

"An excursion!" cried Ned

"We must be going ashore," said Conseil.

I knew that Crespo was a tiny deserted island in the North Pacific, but I had never heard of any forests there.

There was no sign of the captain that day, but the next morning he appeared in the drawing room.

"Ready, gentlemen?" he asked.

We were a little confused because looking out of the drawing room window, we could see that the *Nautilus* had come to a halt on the ocean floor.

The captain saw our confusion. "Don't worry, gentlemen," he said. "You won't be getting wet."

He led us off to an area of the ship beside the engine room. It was a changing room full of diving gear and other equipment. Once more, Captain Nemo had me gasping at the modern technology that he had developed for his own use.

The diving gear and other equipment

I recognized the basic diving suit. But where was the rubber air pipe that linked the diver to his air supply?

"We do not need pipes," he said abruptly. "I have developed a system of compressed air tanks which we carry on our backs. They contain enough air for nine hours. We can walk quite freely wherever we want, until the air runs out."

I was astounded. Next I saw special electric lanterns that were bolted to our huge helmets. They worked by some mysterious battery system. Then there were the guns. I had never seen their like before. They were fired by compressed air. And even more extraordinary was the fact that they fired bullets that were filled with an electrical charge.

"Anyone hit dies as if they had been struck by lightning," Captain Nemo explained.

I asked him about the forest we were to walk in, explaining that I had never heard of forests on the island of Crespo.

"The forests I talk of require neither light, nor heat from the sun," he said. "They are not inhabited by lions and tigers. They are forests that grow under the sea."

Chapter 8
A Stroll on the Ocean Floor

Once we were dressed in our diving suits and helmets, our air tanks were fitted to our backs and turned on. Then I heard a high pitched hissing sound. The doors were locking as our dressing chamber became a tank. Seawater began to pour in from vents in the wall.

The compressed air tanks were working perfectly. We could all breathe easily.

When the water had filled the tank, a door in the hull opened. Captain Nemo led the way, beckoning us to follow.

It seemed very odd, but we just walked out onto the sea bed and followed the captain. It really was just like taking a stroll, though we were on the bottom of the sea.

We were only about thirty feet down and the sun's rays still reached us. Now I could look back and see the full size and shape of the *Nautilus* for the first time. I saw that her hull was made up of overlapping sheets of steel that

Looking back at the Nautilus

looked a little like the protective scales of a fish. Her nose was shaped like the shell of a real nautilus seashell; a spiral of steel that made a murderous-looking battering ram.

Once more Captain Nemo called us on. We followed him on a downward slope. After an hour, we had reached a depth of three hundred feet. Now the rays of the sun were weaker, as if evening had fallen. The captain stopped for a moment and pointed. The underwater forest lay ahead. Soon after, we reached its edge.

The forest consisted of large tree-like plants and bushes. Captain Nemo obviously considered this forest his own. Even in his heavy diving suit, he looked like a gentleman ambling through his own country park.

I saw that Conseil was enchanted by the magic of walking beneath the sea. He didn't seem in the least worried when a three foot tall sea spider galloped out in front of us. I didn't feel so safe. It had horrible squinting eyes and I felt it might pounce on me.

The problem was solved when Captain Nemo shot the sea spider with his compressed air gun. It exploded with a sizzle and hiss, just as if it had been hit by lightning. I wondered what other fearsome animals of the deep were lurking in wait.

Now I was a little concerned about getting back to the *Nautilus*, but Captain Nemo continued on. We were going deeper and deeper into the forest. We entered an underwater valley lying between sheer rock walls, and found our way through it by a narrow path between the trees.

The final light from the sun above had almost gone when Captain Nemo indicated to us to turn on our electric lamps. The lights brilliantly lit up the landscape we were now traveling through.

The forest came to a sudden end in front of a great cliff. It didn't take me long to realize that this was the cliff marking the shoreline of the island of Crespo. We spent a while exploring its base before starting the walk back. Slowly, as we climbed toward the surface again, the natural light returned.

I was starting to feel quite light-headed. Perhaps my air supply was running low.

I was lagging about twenty paces behind when Captain Nemo turned around and rushed back to me. With a violent push, he flung me to the ground. Then he threw himself down beside me.

Deeper and deeper into the forest.

As we lay side by side, I saw two dark shadows pass by. The blood froze in my veins. They were two massive sharks, with enormous jaws and dull, glassy stares.

They didn't see us, but swam on into the distance.

I suddenly realized that the captain had just saved my life. What a strange man he was. Yet, the more I was to get to know him, the stranger he became!

Chapter 9
Grounded!

After we returned to the *Nautilus*, a few more days passed without a sight of Captain Nemo. But early on the morning of November 14, we met again on the platform.

"Professor," he said, "just look at the ocean. Doesn't it have its moods just like us? Yesterday it slept, just like we did. Now it is awakening after a peaceful night."

I didn't need to answer because he was really just talking to himself. He often did.

The next moment, he continued his thoughts. "One day," he said, "I can see great nautical towns and cities – clusters of submarine dwellings which, like the *Nautilus*, would rise to the surface each morning to breathe. Free towns, independent cities!"

During the days that followed, I seldom saw the captain. His appearances were rare. Each day the panels in the drawing room would be opened and Conseil, Ned and myself would spend hours just staring at the amazing under-water world.

And so we traveled on.

We crossed the Tropic of Cancer on November 26. The next day we passed the Hawaiian Islands, although we never came close to the coast. Captain Nemo always put a distance between himself and civilization.

On December 1 we crossed the Equator. The following day Conseil urgently requested my presence in the drawing room. Conseil and Ned were staring out of the window, as the *Nautilus* was resting motionless on the sandy sea bottom.

What an extraordinary sight met my eyes! Outside was a shipwreck. It could only have happened in the last few days. The ship had plunged to its death head-first. Now its nose was firmly stuck in the sand. There was a large circular gash in its side.

It was a warship, probably English. Its sails still fluttered; not in the wind but in the sea currents around it. I saw bodies of seamen caught in those sails, and the helmsman trapped at his wheel. Other victims lay caught under the wreck debris

We stared in silence at the dreadful scene. Had Captain Nemo had anything to do with the ship's sinking? During his disappearances we occasionally heard strange sounds and felt the *Nautilus* shaking as if it had hit something.

Christmas passed with no celebration at all. Ned, a great eater, sorely missed his roast duck. By New Year, we were approaching Australia, with Captain Nemo about to sail through the Torres Strait, to reach the Indian Ocean. The Torres Strait was a dangerous stretch of water, strewn with tiny islands and scores of uncharted rocks.

I was on the platform with the captain. All went well for a while. Then I was suddenly thrown onto the deck. The *Nautilus* had struck a reef and was now motionless.

I got to my feet to find Captain Nemo and his second-in-command talking about the situation quiet calmly.

"Has there been an accident?" I asked.

"Nothing of the kind," he replied, "It was just a small incident. We are temporarily grounded."

"How can you refloat the *Nautilus*?" I asked.

"Today is the fourth day of January," said the captain. "The full moon arrives on the fifth. And with it will come another high tide. The *Nautilus* will be floated off at 2:40 p.m. that day."

He seemed a little irritated that I should

Grounded!

Outside was a shipwreck.

suggest that his beloved *Nautilus* was trapped on the reef. He vanished into the ship.

When I saw Ned, he wasn't convinced that the ship could be freed. "Let me tell you, Professor," he said, "this piece of scrap iron will never set sail again – either on or under the water."

It was then that Ned suggested that I should ask Captain Nemo for permission for all of us to go ashore on a small island that was visible, a few miles off.

"I've had enough of this seafood," he said. "I want to get my teeth into some proper meat. There's bound to be some wild pigs or other animals on the island."

For once, Conseil didn't ask for my approval. He said it would be nice to get our feet on land again.

"I will ask the captain," I said, "but I know he will refuse."

But much to my surprise, Captain Nemo agreed. He even said we could take the *Nautilus'* dinghy and some electric rifles. I suspected the captain thought we might prefer to return to the *Nautilus* rather than face the wild natives who probably lived on the island.

So at eight o'clock the next morning, the dinghy was launched and we set off.

The Nautilus had struck a reef.

"I could eat a horse," said Ned. "And if there are only tigers on the island, I shall eat two of those instead!"

Chapter 10
Ashore

We had now been prisoners of Captain Nemo for two months. We were all delighted to escape the *Nautilus* for a while. Ned and Conseil were even joking about what meat they might find.

"I don't think I shall trust sharing a cabin with you in future," said Conseil. "I think you are in danger of becoming a cannibal with all this talk of needing meat. I fear I'll wake up one morning and find myself half eaten."

"Dear Conseil," said Ned. "I am very fond of you. But not enough to want to eat you!"

It didn't take us long. The island was full of wild pigs and chickens. With Ned's excellent eye for harpooning, he quickly killed a wild pig with his gun. Ned and Conseil built a fire and soon the meat was roasting away. What an excellent dinner that was.

"What do you say that we don't go back to the ship tonight?" suggested Ned, who was always looking for a way to escape.

Just then, a large stone fell between us.

"Savages!" I cried. "No wonder Captain Nemo let us come here!"

We were on our feet in moments and racing for our dinghy. Ned was with us, but not before he had grabbed the remains of the meat.

We dashed for the beach and rowed away from the shore. Soon hundreds of fierce-looking natives had gathered on the beach, watching us escape. Twenty minutes later we safely reached the *Nautilus* and climbed aboard. The ship seemed deserted, but then we heard the sound of organ music coming from below.

We went down into the ship. The captain's cabin door was open and we watched him play the organ. He didn't notice us for a while. His mind seemed miles away

At last he stopped and looked over to us. "Ha! So you have returned," he said. "I thought you might."

"Be warned, Captain," I said. "We met hundreds of savages. You'll need to place guards on the *Nautilus* tonight."

Captain Nemo wasn't at all concerned at my news. "If all the savages from every continent on earth attacked the *Nautilus* at once, there would still be nothing to worry about," he laughed.

"Savages!"

The next morning we saw that dozens of canoes were heading our way. Soon, we were under attack from a hail of arrows. I went below to tell the captain. Once more, he seemed unconcerned.

"I repeat, we are in no danger," he said. "We'll shut the hatches. What can a few arrows do to my ship? Besides, the high tide is due tomorrow. We will be afloat by 2:40 in the afternoon, as promised."

At 2:35 p.m. the next day, Captain Nemo came into the drawing room to tell us that he was about to open the hatches again.

"What about the savages?" I asked.

"What are you worrying about?" he said.

"Surely," I said, "as soon as the hatches are opened, the savages will pour in."

Captain Nemo smiled. "It is not so simple to enter my ship, even when the hatches are open. Come and see."

We followed the captain to the main hatchway. He opened it and dozens of faces appeared above us. The first savage to try and enter put his hand on the metal frame of the hatch and immediately let out a scream of pain.

Others did the same and ran off howling with fear. Conseil was fascinated and put a

He was immediately thrown back.

finger on the hatch. He was immediately thrown back.

"A thousand devils," he cried. "I have been struck by lightning!"

Now I knew why Captain Nemo wasn't worried by the natives. The main entrances to the ship had been wired up to the electricity supply. Anyone touching one would get a nasty electric shock.

We climbed up to the platform, just in time to see the savages rowing away in terror. At that moment I saw one of the ship's clocks. It was now exactly 2:40 on the afternoon of January 5.

There was a slight creak as the *Nautilus* moved on the rising tide and floated off the reef. Without a word, Captain Nemo switched on the propellers and the ship sped away once more. It all happened in the manner and exact time that the captain had said.

The *Nautilus*' propellers thrashed the waters slowly and majestically. Then she gradually picked up speed and sailed smoothly away towards the Timor Sea.

Chapter 11
The Coral Cemetery

Where was Captain Nemo taking us now?

Up until this point, the man had steered clear of the populated corners of the world. Now he seemed to be heading towards the coasts of Asia. Would he dare approach Europe itself?

The journey continued peacefully with few surprises for the next few days.

Captain Nemo was spending more time on the platform than usual. He seemed to be searching the horizon with his telescope for something. A warship?

I went and got a telescope from the drawing room and reappeared on the platform. I was going to search the horizon myself. As soon as Captain Nemo saw me, he snatched the telescope violently from my hands.

I turned to look at him. I no longer recognized his face. His features had been transformed. His eyes lit up menacingly. He gritted his teeth. His body was stiff and his fists clenched. Hatred seemed to fill his whole being, yet still he looked obstinately towards the horizon.

That evening, Conseil, Ned and I were all in the drawing room when the steward arrived with our meal. It included a glass of wine made from some unknown ocean plant. It tasted delicious but soon after, Conseil fell into a deep sleep. Ned was soon unconscious, too.

We had been drugged. I knew it immediately. We were already Captain Nemo's prisoners. What was he hiding from us that required us to be put to sleep? I tried to fight the drug. It was impossible. I too slipped away into unconsciousness.

The next morning we all awoke. Nothing about the ship had changed. The *Nautilus* seemed as quiet and mysterious as ever. I went up onto the platform and scanned the horizon. It was empty as usual.

But that afternoon, Captain Nemo approached me in the drawing room. "Professor Aronnax, are you a doctor?" he asked.

I replied that I had studied medicine for many years before joining the Museum of Natural History in Paris.

"In that case," he said, "would you be kind

Hatred seemed to fill his whole being.

enough to come and have a look at one of my men?"

"Of course," I said.

He led me to a cabin, where a man lay on his bed. He had a horrendous wound on his head.

"Where did he get that?" I asked.

"It's nothing to do with you," he muttered. "It was just an accident in the engine room. Just tell me if he will live."

I examined the man and quickly saw that he was fatally wounded. "This man will die within two hours," I replied. "Nothing can save him."

Then I saw the most amazing thing. Tears formed in Captain Nemo's eyes. I had never thought him capable of showing emotion. He seemed to have an extraordinary loyalty and feeling towards each member of his crew.

There was something special that bound the captain and his crew together. It was as if they belonged to each other, and were a kind of family . . .

I left him with the dying man and went to my cabin.

The next morning I went up onto the platform and met Captain Nemo again.

"Would you and your friends like to take another journey under the sea today?" he asked.

"Nothing can save him."

"Of course," I said enthusiastically.

"Then go and put on your diving suits and get ready," he said.

We were ready by eight o'clock. Once more the hull door opened and we walked out onto the sea floor. We found ourselves in the wonderland of a coral reef. We switched on our lights and followed Captain Nemo, and some of his crew.

We walked for about two hours and reached a depth of some nine hundred feet. We were now in a great clearing surrounded by the skeletons of coral and dead trees. It was a truly haunting place.

Suddenly, Captain Nemo and the crew with him stopped. One of the men stepped forward with a pickaxe and started to dig a hole in the coral. I looked around and saw that there were lots of small areas where the coral had been dug up. Small piles of broken coral covered raised areas of ground.

Soon after, a further six of the crew arrived, carrying the body of the man I had seen the day before. The truth hit me. This was an underwater cemetery.

At last I understood the purpose of our journey. The captain and his men had come to bury a comrade in this communal resting ground at the very bottom of the ocean.

The dead man was laid in his grave and covered with coral. Captain Nemo and his crew knelt in prayer. They were saying a final farewell to a comrade. The ceremony moved me greatly.

That night the captain spoke to me. "That man is now at rest with his companions in the coral cemetery. We will never forget him."

"Your dead sleep quietly there," I said, "well beyond the reach of sharks."

The wonderland of a coral reef.

"Yes, monsieur," he replied. "Beyond the reach of sharks . . . and of men!"

It was clear to me now that Captain Nemo hoped he would one day be buried in that coral cemetery himself, far from the reach of other men. Neither sea monster nor man would ever trouble his last sleep in the peace of this very special place on earth.

Chapter 12
The Giant Pearl

After the funeral, I couldn't help wondering if Captain Nemo used the *Nautilus* for more than just touring the ocean depths. Where did he go when he vanished for days on end?

Why had he snatched the telescope from me? Why had Conseil, Ned and I been drugged?

Whatever the real reason, it seemed to me that the captain wasn't as open about his true activities as he pretended. He might show me some of the secrets of the Nautilus, yet, there were other things he didn't want me to see.

How had that crewman been mortally wounded? Had the captain been looking for a ship? Had the crewman been injured in an assault on that ship? The fact remained that we were prisoners and unlikely to ever find out.

Ned and Conseil had not given up hope of being freed, or escaping. Yet, for myself, I had the strangest wish to finish this extraordinary voyage and discover the secrets of Captain Nemo and his crew.

The captain was now driving the *Nautilus* hard. Between January 21 and 23, the ship averaged five hundred and forty miles a day. On January 26 we crossed the Equator again, heading towards India, and the Bay of Bengal. Once more we were in the Northern Hemisphere.

Two days later we surfaced with land in sight.

"Tonight," said Captain Nemo, "we are going hunting again."

Then without another word, he was gone. "What now?" I wondered.

That night we left the *Nautilus* in our diving suits. It wasn't long before I saw our prey . . . precious pearl oysters. There seemed to be hundreds of them. Captain Nemo gathered a few bags full but then led us ever deeper.

At last, we reached a great rocky cavern. Inside, attached to the wall, was a gigantic oyster. It was the largest I had ever seen and must have weighed more than six hundred pounds.

Captain Nemo beckoned to me. I approached the oyster. The two halves of the shell were open. Now I saw it. Inside was a

We surfaced, with land in sight.

sparkling pearl, bigger than a coconut. I wanted to try and pick it up.

The captain saw my intention and pulled me away. The oyster quickly slammed shut. Captain Nemo indicated that he didn't want the pearl touched. It was obvious that he had seen this great pearl before and wanted it protected from the prying eyes of bounty hunters.

More importantly still, he probably wanted the pearl to grow even larger. Only then would he pluck his priceless fruit and add it to his incredible collection of sea rarities, paintings and other priceless objects in the museum of the *Nautilus*.

A few minutes later, as we made our way back to the surface, we saw a shadow dropping to the bottom of the sea. For a moment, I thought it was a shark. But it was only a pearl diver; a man who made his living by collecting pearls from the sea bed.

The diver could not see us. We were hidden by some rocks. Repeatedly, he dived down with a rope around his waist and a rock held between his feet, to help him sink more quickly. I could see the shadow of his boat above us.

On each dive he gathered up as many as

The Giant Pearl

A sparkling pearl

ten pearl oysters before running out of breath and returning to the surface. If only he had known how close he was to that giant pearl! It would have made him a wealthy man, who would never again have to dive into the dangers of the deep.

Just then, as he dived again, I saw another shadow follow him down. This time it *was* a shark. The diver saw the great fish and dodged its first attack, but he couldn't avoid the violent swish of the creature's tail. It struck him on the chest and threw him flat on the ocean floor.

The shark was about to attack again when I saw Captain Nemo suddenly get up, with his dagger in hand. He walked towards the monster shark, ready to fight it single-handedly.

The shark saw the captain and turned to attack him. As the creature lunged at him, he stepped aside with incredible speed. He avoided the shark's razor-sharp teeth by inches. At the same time, he plunged his dagger into the belly of the monster. Blood poured from the wound and the waters turned red. It was hard to see what happened next.

Captain Nemo was clinging onto one of the shark's fins. The beast was in its death throes, yet it was turning and about to make one last

The Giant Pearl

Walking towards the monster shark

fatal snap. The captain's death seemed certain. The shark's jaws opened wide . . .

Suddenly, something hit the shark with enormous force. It was Ned's harpoon. There was no more accurate a harpooner in the world, and Ned's thrust had saved the captain at the very last moment. Captain Nemo just nodded, hardly acknowledging that Ned had saved his life.

Then something odd happened. The captain got to his feet and went over the diver who was now recovering but running desperately short of breath. What must the diver have thought, to see these strange creatures around him?

Captain Nemo pulled a bag of pearls from his own pocket and thrust them into the diver's own bag. Then, with all his strength, he pushed the man towards the surface. The last I saw of the young man were his startled eyes as he stared at his rescuers from another world.

That evening, safely back aboard the *Nautilus*, I wondered about the great courage of the captain. Who else would have dared defend another's life against a man-eating shark? A jailer? Pirate? Brave man? Misunderstood genius? Captain Nemo seemed as deep and complex as the oceans he haunted.

I did ask him why he had given the man a bag of pearls.

"That diver is an ordinary man – a simple man," was his reply. "He risks his life every day to earn a living, just to keep his family alive. Surely he deserves a little help, when the rich and powerful plunder the world for their own gain, and think little of the poor."

Captain Nemo clearly supported the world's underdogs.

Chapter 13
The Tunnel

The *Nautilus* now turned east, and into the Arabian Sea. I noticed that the dials in the drawing room indicated that we had traveled 16,220 miles, or 7,500 leagues, since leaving the coast near Japan.

We had been prisoners on the *Nautilus* for nearly three months.

It now looked as if we were heading for the Persian Gulf. That confused Ned.

"Where on earth are we going?" he asked.

"Master Ned," I replied, "we are going where the captain's whims take us. That's all I can say."

"But the Persian Gulf is a dead end," said Ned. "We will just have to come back out again."

"Then we will have to come back out," I said, "and then we may go into the Red Sea."

"That's also a dead end," said Ned. "Perhaps he wants to wait there until the Suez Canal is finished and opened, in two years' time. Then

"Where on earth are we going?"

he can proceed straight into the Mediterranean Sea."

None of us could even guess what the captain intended. It only increased Ned's desire to escape. He was praying that the captain would take the *Nautilus* near enough to the European coastline to achieve it.

Ned's firm belief was simple. "One cannot be happy," he said, "unless one is free."

I wasn't so sure. And our next adventure only convinced me further that I didn't want to leave the *Nautilus* too quickly.

Captain Nemo did sail into the Persian Gulf and then retraced his steps. After this, we sailed south into the Red Sea. The next day we saw the small town of Suez ahead of us. This was to be the southern end of the Suez Canal, when it was completed.

"It's a pity that the Suez Canal isn't finished," I said to the captain. "We could have sailed straight into the Mediterranean."

"I agree, it is unfortunate that I can't take you through the Suez Canal," he replied. "Nevertheless the *Nautilus* and all of us will be in the Mediterranean Sea by tomorrow morning."

"Impossible!" I cried. "To get to the Mediterranean, you would have to sail right around Africa and north, to Gibraltar. That would take weeks."

"Professor," he said, "what makes you think that the *Nautilus* is going around Africa?"

"How else?" I answered. "Unless this marvelous ship of yours can sail on dry land, across the Egyptian deserts."

"How about sailing under it," smiled Captain Nemo.

"Under it!" I exclaimed.

"You will not have heard of what I call the Arabian Tunnel," he replied calmly. "No one else has. I am the only man on earth who knows of it; the only man who has seen it."

"A tunnel?" I gasped. "You mean to say there is an unknown tunnel that leads from the Red Sea and comes out in the Mediterranean Sea?"

"Indeed," said Captain Nemo. "And seeing that you will never be free to leave my ship to reveal my secret, I will show it to you."

"How did you find the tunnel?" I asked.

"Simple," he said. "I noticed that the same types of fish lived in both the Red Sea and the Mediterranean Sea. I guessed there had to be a subterranean tunnel, to make this possible."

The captain explained how he had caught lots of the fish in the Red Sea and marked them by attaching small copper rings to their tails. He had then returned them to the water.

"A few months later," he continued, "I caught several of those fish in the southern Mediterranean. So that proved my point. After searching for several weeks, I found the entrance. I have sailed through it several times now. Join me on the platform tomorrow and you shall see."

I told Ned and Conseil about what the captain had told me. They didn't believe a word of it.

They were still sleeping when I joined Captain Nemo at dawn on the platform, the next morning.

"You are an honored guest today," he said. "You will be by my side in the steering cage for the next part of the journey."

There was only just room in the steering cage for myself, the captain and the helmsman. I only prayed that the reinforced glass would be strong enough to protect us from the water pressure as we submerged.

"Take us down, Helmsman," ordered Captain Nemo.

The *Nautilus* slipped gracefully beneath the surface and increased speed. We dived for

"Take us down, Helmsman."

several hundred feet before leveling out and entering a vast cavern. Ahead, I saw what looked like an undersea waterfall. Little was I to know then, that this was the meeting place of the waters of the Red Sea and Mediterranean Sea.

The *Nautilus* put on her lights as she was quickly swept up in the swirling waters and pushed deeper into the cavern. Captain Nemo put his ship's engines into full reverse to retain control over the powerful current.

Very soon, though, we reached quieter waters which swept us along more gently. The cavern now became a much narrower tunnel. The helmsman had his work cut out to avoid hitting the tunnel's walls, worn smooth by millions of years of erosion.

So we crept northwards. Gradually I could see the waters start to grow lighter. Daylight lay ahead. Another few minutes and we came out of the tunnel and surfaced. We were in the Mediterranean Sea!

It had taken us less than half an hour to travel from the Red Sea to the Mediterranean Sea. I couldn't believe it.

Chapter 14
Volcano!

Soon after surfacing in the Mediterranean Sea, Ned and Conseil appeared on the platform.

"Well, Monsieur," said Ned, "where is the Mediterranean you were talking about?"

"You are cruising on it right now," I said, smiling.

"I don't believe a word of it," was the reply.

"See that coastline," I said. "That town there is Port Said. And Port Said is on the Mediterranean Sea, in Egypt."

"Never!" said Ned.

Conseil gave an expected answer. "If Monsieur says it is Egypt, then it is Egypt."

Ned looked closely at the town on the horizon. It was then that he recognized some of the buildings of Port Said.

"Well," he said, "if we have come through an unknown tunnel overnight, and if we are in the Mediterranean, then I have only one thing to say. We are now in Europe again and should make our escape as soon as possible, before Captain Nemo drags us back to some watery grave in the Pacific."

For the first time, I told Ned how I really felt. "I am reluctant to join you," I said. "The captain has opened my eyes to so many secrets of the deep; I'd hate to miss any other opportunities he might give me. Maybe we should stay with the *Nautilus* until the end of the journey."

"And when, or where, is the end?" asked Ned.

"I have no idea," I replied.

"I'm sure Captain Nemo will free us at some time," said Conseil.

"Doubtful," I said. "We know many of his secrets, and I don't think he would want us to reveal them to the world."

"Well, I still think we should keep an eye open for an escape, whatever you say!" said Ned.

Reluctantly, I knew he was talking sense. However much I wanted to stay, I knew that Captain Nemo's behavior was far too erratic to wish to stay aboard forever. Finally, I agreed with him that if a real chance of escape appeared, then we should take it.

"But we must make sure that we are successful in the first attempt," I warned. "If Captain

"That town there is Port Said."

Nemo finds out, he will never forgive us. He'll lock us away forever, or feed us to the sharks."

"Our best chance will always be the dinghy," said Ned. "We could free the bolts on the hatch and rise to the surface. The pilot in his cage probably wouldn't even see us go."

"Remember what I have said, Ned," I warned again. "I have no doubt that Captain Nemo will be especially on his guard while we are in European waters."

"Our best chance will always be the dinghy."

Over the next few days, Captain Nemo kept the *Nautilus* mostly below the surface. When the ship did rise, it was usually to take on fresh air. Then it sank again, as quickly as possible. The captain spent a lot of the time in the drawing room, watching the Mediterranean pass by. I wondered what was on his mind.

Then one morning looking out, I saw a diver just outside the drawing room window. I assumed he was in trouble.

"Captain," I cried. "A diver! We must rescue him."

Captain Nemo didn't reply, but waved to the man as if signaling a friend. The man swam off, back towards the surface.

"Don't worry," he said, as if the appearance of a diver outside was an everyday happening. "It's only Nicholas. They call him 'The Fish'. He spends his life in the sea. He is a friend."

Captain Nemo turned to a huge chest, which was bound with iron strips. It had the word *Nautilus* marked on the top. I had often wondered what was in it.

The captain took out a key and opened the chest. The glow of gold met my eyes; it was full of gold ingots. I knew they could be worth nothing less than many millions of dollars, and could hardly believe my eyes. A little later, four crewmen appeared and took the chest away.

Next, I heard the pumps of the *Nautilus* starting up. We were surfacing. Then I heard the dinghy being launched. Two hours later it returned, and the *Nautilus* sank to the depths of the ocean once more.

It was quite clear to me that those millions of dollars worth of gold had been delivered to someone. Who? Perhaps the diver who I had seen.

I related the events to Ned and Conseil. "Where does Captain Nemo get these millions?" asked Ned.

I couldn't answer his question. At that moment I was more concerned about how hot it had suddenly become. The sweat was beginning to drip from my face.

Just then, the captain entered. "A bit warm, eh?" he said.

"Is there a fire somewhere?" I asked.

"No," he replied, "but we are sailing through a current of boiling water."

Outside the drawing room window, I saw that the seawater was bubbling. And, behind the bubbles, I could see a reddish glow.

"Where are we?" I asked.

The seawater was bubbling.

"We are close to a submerged but still live volcano," said Captain Nemo. "I thought you might enjoy the visit."

Indeed, despite the heat, I was fascinated. It was these moments that tempted me to stay with the captain forever. Who else on the planet had ever seen a live underwater volcano, or any of the other incredible things that Captain Nemo had shown me on this journey?

The heat was becoming unbearable. I could actually see the scarlet flames from the volcano shooting up through the water. At last, the captain gave the order to move on. Within minutes we were traveling through cooler waters, and the temperature dropped.

What an amazing experience. I was just glad that Ned hadn't taken the chance to escape during our visit to the underwater volcano.

We would all have been burnt alive.

Chapter 15
The Captain's Treasure

It was evident that Captain Nemo had no love for the Mediterranean Sea. It was surrounded by those same countries that he was fleeing, for whatever reason.

One man who did like the Mediterranean was Conseil. He had been with me for several years and had learned much about the natural world. While he did not, perhaps, understand a great deal, he had become excellent at classifying creatures and noting their names.

His constant companion was a huge notebook in which he listed every single creature he saw. Most of their names were unpronounceable, even to me.

Lampreys, oxyrrhyncha, conger eels, flying gurnards, triggerfish, flounder, cachalot, white-bellied seals, spiny oysters, corrugated cockles, sea-ears, wedge shells, sea hares, spider crabs, amphipods, isopods and trilobites . . .

Conseil's list was getting longer by the day. He was becoming very inquisitive about scientific affairs and one day, he asked me how long the sun would keep the world warm.

"Some day, it will die," I said. "It will run out of gas to burn. It will become as cold and lifeless as the moon."

"But how long before that happens?" he asked.

"Many millions of years, perhaps," I replied.

"Well," he said, "we have more than enough time to complete our journey . . . unless, of course, Ned Land messes things up."

I smiled. Conseil was now on my side. He was rather more interested in listing more exotic creatures than escaping.

Certainly, Ned was a million times keener than either of us to escape.

***

It only took us two days to cross the Mediterranean. By February 17 we were approaching the Straits of Gibraltar.

Once more I spent a lot of time by the drawing room window. What tragedies I saw lying all around that area; rotting warships,

Conseil's list was getting longer by the day.

rusting chains, cannonballs and cannons. The seabed was littered with bones from a hundred shipwrecks.

The next day we sailed out of the Mediterranean and into the Atlantic Ocean.

At last Captain Nemo allowed the *Nautilus* to fully surface again. I was able to enjoy the view, and the fresh air from the platform once more.

But I was worried, too. Ned came to me that first morning into the Atlantic. "Our escape,"

What tragedies I saw!

he announced, "is all set for tonight!"

I tried to object, but he rightly recalled that I had promised to support an escape.

"We are as close as we'll ever get to France," he said. "The Spanish coast is still visible. The wind is set fair to blow us to shore. The dinghy is just waiting for us."

What could I say? It was madness to stay with Captain Nemo, despite all the attractions of the voyage.

"Okay, Ned," I said. "What's your plan?"

"I shall prepare the dinghy," he said, "while you wait in the drawing room for me to come and get you. We board the dinghy in darkness. By the time they know we have gone, the *Nautilus* will be miles away."

I remained in my cabin for the rest of the day, just in case I met Captain Nemo and my face showed what I was thinking.

Since the night when the dinghy had left the ship with the gold, I increasingly wondered if the captain did go ashore during those periods when he went missing.

Was he a spy? Was he carrying out secret missions for some foreign government? Or did he really roam the oceans to escape mankind?

The more I thought about it, the more

puzzled I became. That evening I went to my room and put on warm clothes for the adventure ahead. Then I went to the drawing room, to await Ned and Conseil.

No sooner had I arrived than the *Nautilus* stopped and Captain Nemo came in.

"We are in Vigo Bay," he said calmly. "I have a little history lesson for you."

The drawing room panels drew back. It was dark outside.

The captain told me how on October 12, 1702 the greatest-ever fleet of Spanish gold bullion ships was nearing the end of its journey at this place, when it was attacked by some English ships. He said that rather than lose the gold to the English, the Spanish admiral ordered all his ships to be sunk.

Now the captain switched on the ship's searchlights. What an extraordinary sight. The whole area was littered with broken chests and the seabed was a mass of gold bars.

Very soon after, I saw some of Captain Nemo's crew in diving gear, collecting gold bars. At last, I saw where his fortune came from.

"You see," he said, "all I do is harvest what other men have lost or left behind. There are thousands of sites around the world like this;

At last, I saw where his fortune came from.

gold and silver in untold quantities, just waiting to be collected. I don't need to raise it all at once. I simply stop the *Nautilus* and refill my coffers when necessary."

I explained that I could see how he might need a lot of money to build and run the *Nautilus*. But why did he need so very much? "Money isn't everything," I said.

"Do you think I am greedy?" shouted the captain, angrily. "Do you think I harvest these riches just for my own benefit? Isn't it possible that I use my fortune for good?"

I realized I had said something that really annoyed him.

"I am well aware that there are human beings in this world who are suffering; people who are oppressed by cruel men, people who need to be comforted, victims who need to be avenged. Monsieur le Professor, don't you understand?" he continued.

I could see that whatever reasons had driven Captain Nemo to lead an independent life beneath the sea, he was still a feeling man. He had emotions. Deep down, his heart still belonged to the human race.

I guessed that the gold ingots I had heard leaving the ship earlier had gone to help some worthy cause connected with the diver we had seen.

Someone in need of comfort at that moment was Ned. Immediately the *Nautilus* had stopped, he knew the planned escape had to be cancelled. Any success had depended on the ship traveling at speed, to give us time to get well away before anyone realized we had gone.

In my heart of hearts, I was glad.

Chapter 16

Visit to the Lost Continent

The next morning the *Nautilus* got underway again. But much to Ned's disappointment, he saw that Captain Nemo had changed direction.

The *Nautilus* was now heading south. She had turned her back on Europe. The hatches were all closed and locked. Captain Nemo was not to be seen either. Any idea of an escape was now out of the question.

The captain reappeared a few days later. "I have another adventure for you," he announced. "Be ready in your diving suit this evening."

This time neither Conseil nor Ned were invited.

That evening the *Nautilus* stopped, and Captain Nemo and I set off. The waters were pitch-black, but there was a reddish glow in the distance. We turned on our helmet lights to see the way.

Soon after starting out, I tripped on something that looked very much like a low pile of

There was a reddish glow in the distance.

stones. They puzzled me. They looked too regular to have been left by nature.

As we walked, I began to wonder if Captain Nemo was taking me to meet some of his friends; other men who had turned their backs on the world.

An hour later, I saw that the ever-brightening glow was coming from behind an undersea mountain. Looking back I could see that the lights of the *Nautilus* had now disappeared.

We were a long way from our mother ship. I wasn't worried, though, as I had confidence in the captain. As I watched him lead the way, I thought how much he looked like a true spirit of the sea, walking boldly toward the red horizon.

It was one o'clock in the morning by the time we reached the lower slopes of the mountain, and entered a forest of dead trees. The oddest thing was that we seemed to be walking up some sort of mountain track; a once well-used track, at that.

But for the fifty feet of water above our heads, we might have been walking up a mountain track anywhere on earth.

Two hours after leaving the *Nautilus*, we were close to the top of the mountain. The red glow behind was brighter than ever. What strange, fantastic world was Captain Nemo taking me into?

As we approached the top, I was astounded to see the remains of some buildings. I wanted to stop and examine them but Captain Nemo indicated that we should keep going. At last, we reached the summit.

We were met by a blinding red glow. The light came from a distant but still very live volcano. It took a few moments for me to regain my sight. Then I saw it. Between me and the volcano was a great plain. And lying on that plain were the ruins of a vast submerged city.

It was a shattered city. There wasn't a single house with its roof in place. Huge temples had collapsed in heaps of rubble. All the streets were blocked by fallen debris. It was like seeing the empty streets of Pompeii after Mount Vesuvius had destroyed that once-great city.

I saw where a sandy beach had been; a place where one day the tide had come in and never gone out again. I realized from the size and magnificence of the buildings that this was once one of the greatest cities of all time.

So this was what Captain Nemo had brought me to see. But where was I? Where could all this be? I had to know. If only I could speak to the captain! He must have known what I was thinking. He picked up a piece of chalk from the ground and walked across to a dark rock. On that rock he scribbled one word:

ATLANTIS

I was astonished. This was Atlantis, the capital of the Lost Continent! There it was before my very eyes; the sight that historians had yearned to see for two thousand years or more.

This was the main city of the long-lost continent of Atlantis that linked America to Europe; a continent destroyed by earthquake and that glowing volcano in the distance.

I stood there dreaming, trying to fix into my mind the detail of the scene. Captain Nemo was leaning on a broken pillar. He was clearly enjoying my excitement at the vision below. Was this where he came sometimes, to try and puzzle out the secret of human destiny?

How I wanted to descend from the mountain and walk those ruined streets. But the captain gently waved his hand to indicate that there was little time left. Our air would soon be running short.

It was a shattered city.

Just then, the rays of the moon broke through the surface of the water above. They cast pale shadows across the submerged continent. The scene was indescribably beautiful.

Captain Nemo motioned to me to follow him back. We descended the mountain and retraced our steps. We reached the *Nautilus* just as the sun was rising. I was exhausted by the journey, but excited by some of the most extraordinary scenes I had ever witnessed in my life.

Chapter 17
Southbound

Ned could not believe I had seen Atlantis when I met him the next day.

Of course, Conseil did.

"If Monsieur says he has been to the lost continent of Atlantis," he said, "then Monsieur has been. As for me, today I have added a sea dragon, swordfish, prickly dolphin, tunnyfish, telescope fish, an armored marmalat and a grenadier fish to my list."

"Your list is becoming a work that future scientists will value greatly," I said, winking at Ned.

In the days that followed, we realized that Captain Nemo was heading into the vast emptiness of the South Atlantic. He seemed more relaxed, once the *Nautilus* had passed out of the busy North Atlantic shipping lanes.

More relaxed yes, but not any happier. Often I heard him in his cabin playing sad music on his organ.

It was now March and we had traveled more than 13,000 leagues since our capture. One day Captain Nemo, perhaps a little bored, sent the *Nautilus* into a steep dive. An hour later, the ship reached 43,000 feet. Still, the *Nautilus* dived.

How she coped with the pressures I will never know. I felt the ship's steel plates vibrate. Its bulkheads quivered. The window in the drawing room appeared to bulge under the pressure.

Soon we were below the level marking the limits of much marine life. We had reached the 50,000 feet mark. The hull of the ship was now bearing a pressure of 24,000 pounds on every square inch of its surface.

"An incredible experience!" I said to Captain Nemo. "We are traveling in places no other man on earth has seen. No man has been deeper than this."

Soon after, the captain ordered the ship to return to the surface. "We must not abuse our power," he said. "We mustn't expose the *Nautilus* to such pressures for too long. Hold on tight!"

I just had time to grab a safety rail before the *Nautilus* went into an almost vertical climb. She emerged on the surface a few moments later, like a flying fish.

Still, the Nautilus dived.

That evening Captain Nemo retired and I sat with Conseil and Ned to talk about my extraordinary journey to the lost continent of Atlantis. As we talked, it became clear that Ned wasn't happy. The long months of imprisonment in the *Nautilus* were taking their toll on him.

Ned was a naturally aggressive man and often his eyes lit up in anger when he came face-to-face with his jailer, Captain Nemo. It didn't help when one day, he spotted several whales from the drawing room window. He asked the captain's permission to go and hunt them down. Ned, after all, was a professional whale hunter and the best harpooner in the business.

"Just one whale?" asked the captain.

"Why, no," said Ned. "There are plenty. I could kill several with my harpoons."

Captain Nemo stared back angrily. "If all whalers like you have their way," he said, "one day in the future you will wipe out the last whale alive."

Ned's hostility to the captain only increased after that incident.

Fortunately, the weather soon helped to cool his hot temper. We were heading south at speed. On March 14, I noticed floating ice. Was Captain Nemo heading for the South Pole?

The further south we traveled, the more ice we saw. Soon we were among a myriad of ice islands. The temperature had fallen to around three degrees below zero. On March 16 we crossed the Antarctic Circle. Very soon after, we found our way blocked by mountainous areas of ice. We had almost reached the continent of Antarctica.

The ice didn't stop the *Nautilus*. She battered her way on like an icebreaker. The power of the ship blasted great lumps of ice into the air. They

"Just one whale?"

scenery beneath the ice. Poor Conseil. His list of creatures only increased by two: a seal and a walrus!

On the evening of the second day the *Nautilus* stopped and began to rise. I watched from the drawing room, expecting the ship to emerge onto the surface of a polar sea. But no! A sudden shock made me realize that the *Nautilus* had struck the underside of the ice. I looked at the dials and saw that we were still at a depth of some three thousand feet.

The South Pole was clearly somewhere above our heads. What would the captain do now?

Chapter 18
The South Pole

It was soon clear that Captain Nemo was going to use the sheer strength of the *Nautilus* to batter his way to the surface. Time and time again, the ship rose rapidly and crashed into the ice above. Moving forward and upwards, the work went on all day. The light from above became brighter with each charge.

At last, by late evening, the final few feet of ice gave way. We emerged into a world of frozen wastes. A blinding snowstorm prevented the captain from taking a navigational reading from the sun, to see whether we had actually reached the South Pole.

There was nothing he could do but wait impatiently in the *Nautilus* for it to pass.

The next day the sun returned, allowing Captain Nemo to take his reading from a slight hillock of ice. A few moments later I saw a strange expression cross his face. It was not just a smile, but a look of power and madness in one.

"For hundreds of years Man has tried to reach the South Pole," he began. "But they never could. Now on March 21, 1868, I, Captain Nemo, have done what no other man could do. My reading confirms that this is the exact position of the South Pole."

His eyes were open wide and staring now. His hands were shaking as he continued. "I am taking possession of this land . . ."

I interrupted him at this historic moment. "In whose name?" I asked.

"Mine, of course," he said matter-of-factly.

Captain Nemo unfurled a black banner, bearing the letter *N* embroidered in gold.

Then he turned towards the sun, whose last rays were dying on the horizon. "Farewell, sun," he cried, "Rest beneath the open sea. And let the shadows of the long night fall on my new ice kingdom."

For the first time, the captain truly frightened me. I knew there was a terrifying streak of madness in him.

The lesser madness of Conseil found my faithful servant with plenty of new creatures to list, including a penguin, a long-legged wader belonging to the pigeon family, an albatross and a petrel.

Taking a navigational reading

The next day, March 22, at ten o'clock in the evening, the *Nautilus* left the South Pole and set off north with the Southern Cross, the polar group of stars, glittering down on us. We had now been aboard the ship for five and a half months, and traveled 14,000 leagues.

The following night as I was sleeping, I was jolted awake by a massive shock. I was thrown into the middle of my cabin and I felt the ship heel over at a steep angle.

I clambered out into the corridor, where I met Ned and Conseil.

"What's happened?" I asked.

"The *Nautilus* has hit something," said Ned, "and I don't think she'll get out of this as easily as she did the last collision."

Soon after, Captain Nemo came to explain what had happened. An iceberg as big as a small mountain had turned over and sunk, hitting the ship as it went down and rolling underneath us. "The iceberg is now rising again," he said, "and pushing us up with it."

Just then, there was a loud grinding sound. The captain managed to open the drawing room panels and we saw our awful position.

Above us was a ceiling of ice. Beneath us, the iceberg was still pushing up and around us. We

I was jolted awake.

127

were trapped in a kind of ice tunnel. Our way ahead was blocked by ice. So was our way down and sideways. Our only way out was to reverse.

Captain Nemo quickly ordered the steersman to reverse. Yet another collision was felt. It sent us all tumbling to the ground. Parts of the iceberg had formed yet another barrier, this time behind us.

"That's it," said Ned. "We are truly trapped with nowhere to go."

He was right. We were now prisoners beneath the ice.

Chapter 19
Trapped Beneath the Ice

Captain Nemo looked grim. "There are two
ways for us to die now," he said. "We may be
crushed to death as we are squeezed up against
the ice above. Or else we can be asphyxiated
when the air runs out. We have but a day's
supply."

"Is there any hope of escape?" I asked.

"The ice above us and to the sides is very
thick," he said. "Our only chance is to attack the
ice beneath us; dig a trench as wide and as long
as the ship itself. If we can dig deep enough, we
can use the power of the *Nautilus* to smash a
path through to the open sea beneath us."

The captain said he had already sent out a
team of divers to begin work. A few moments
later we saw them appear outside the drawing
room window and start to attack the ice
beneath us.

"We will keep digging in teams until we
escape or die," he said.

The work was to be done in shifts. Two hours later Captain Nemo, Conseil, Ned and I replaced the first team outside.

It was brutal work, hacking away at the ice with pickaxes. Progress was slow and exhausting. It seemed that for every foot we dug through the ice, another foot of ice froze behind us.

"We will never cut through at this rate," said Ned.

The captain reluctantly agreed. "Professor," he said, "we will need a miracle now if we are not to be entombed in this ice forever. And the air will begin to run out tomorrow."

Suddenly, a look of hope crossed his face and he began to smile. It was then that I heard him utter two words: "Boiling water!"

"Pardon, Captain?" I asked.

"We can use the power of the ship's hot water tanks to speed up the process of removing the ice," he said, excitedly. "We can attack the ice by pumping out hot water!"

A brilliant idea indeed. But would it work?

Every available means of heating water was quickly put to work. The captain himself stood at the pump, ready for the first supply. It was now a race against time. The ship's air was

Attacking the ice beneath us

quickly vanishing, especially with the divers working outside needing so much.

Captain Nemo fired the first burst of boiling water at the shallow ice trench that had already been dug beneath the ship. It worked well, but very slowly. By dawn the next morning, more than twenty feet of ice had been melted or hacked out.

The air inside the ship was now almost poisonous. We all preferred to be outside digging or working the pump. But the work was so exhausting we had to come inside to rest eventually.

During the morning it became worse. Inside the ship, we were all starting to gasp for breath. A few of us were all but unconscious.

"If only I could stop breathing," said the noble Conseil, "there would be more air for you to breathe, Monsieur."

To hear him speak like that brought tears to my eyes.

Work outside went on at a desperate pace. Our lives depended on it. By afternoon, hardly a breath of air remained in the *Nautilus*. I felt dizzy and sick. My lungs were screaming for fresh air.

Now there was no time left. Another half an

hour and we would all be dead. There was no more air, even for the divers.

Captain Nemo took desperate measures. With virtually his last breath, he called everyone back into the ship. Then he ordered a series of violent movements of the ship. His plan was to wriggle out of the icy tomb.

First the ship crashed forward a few inches. And then backwards. Then sideways. Inch by inch, he found the *Nautilus* a little space to move. Now he ordered full diving thrust. Could the ship break through the remaining ice beneath us?

Once, twice and three times the ship pounded on the ice. We waited. We gasped what we thought must be our last breath. Suddenly the ice gave way. The *Nautilus* shot down through the ice!

"Full power ahead!" cried the captain.

The *Nautilus* powered ahead, changing direction so that its nose pointed up at a sharp degree, towards the upper ice levels.

"More power!" screamed Captain Nemo, to the engine room. "Give me everything the ship has got!"

The *Nautilus* charged forwards and upwards, ready to hurl herself at the ice.

Suddenly the ice gave way.

I was gasping. My lungs were bursting. Then the ship hit the ice like a giant arrow. Once more, we were sent tumbling at the impact.

But the power of that extraordinary ship was enough. The surface ice split apart and the *Nautilus* crashed through to the open air once more. The hatches were opened and fresh air flooded into the ship.

Chapter 20
The Giant Squid

We were all in happy mood when the *Nautilus* began sailing north again; away from the nightmare of being trapped in the ice. On March 31 we passed Cape Horn and the southern tip of the American continent. The next day we surfaced near Tierra del Fuego and then proceeded to the Falkland Islands.

By April 4 we were off Uruguay and still sailing north. A week later we passed the mouth of the Amazon River, giving Conseil the chance to jot down on his list such exotica as the unpronounceable '*pteromyzons-pricka fish*' and little-known '*fishbat*'.

One day, Conseil even managed to get stung by a monster ray that Ned had just caught, when he was examining it.

"I shall have my revenge on that ray," he said.

"How?" I asked.

"If Monsieur permits," he replied, "by eating it!"

He did eat it too, even though it was as tough as leather.

By April 20 we were close to the Bahamas. We were diving at about 5,000 feet when we saw lots of mysterious caves in a cliff face. They were so deep that even our most powerful searchlights couldn't pierce the darkness inside them. We also noticed that the sea creatures in this part of the world seemed much larger than elsewhere.

The caves and the sea creatures reminded Conseil of something. "I clearly remember

"I shall have my revenge on that ray."

seeing a huge squid drag a large ship beneath the waves," he said.

"I don't believe you," said Ned. "Where did you see that?"

"In a church," laughed Conseil. "It was in a painting."

I had heard about that painting and knew that its subject was based on a famous legend about a giant squid.

"I think it was just a tall story," said Ned.

"I'm not so sure," I replied. "I once saw the body of a giant octopus in France. "And a sea captain called Bouger reported seeing a squid about twenty feet long. They called it *Bouguer's Squid*. Now wouldn't you like to be able to jot that one down in your list, Conseil!"

Conseil, who had been looking out of the drawing room window, asked a question. "Did *Bouguer's Squid* have eight tentacles that splashed in the water like a nest of snakes?"

"I believe so," I replied.

"And were its eyes huge, and set near the top of its head?"

"I believe so," I answered again.

"And did it have a mouth just like an enormous parrot's beak?"

"Indeed," said I.

"Well," said Conseil, "if Monsieur doesn't mind me saying so, if what I'm looking at now is not *Bouguer's Squid*, it must be one of its brothers. Look!"

Ned and I turned to the drawing room window. What an astonishing and horrific sight met our eyes! Just outside the window was a giant squid, at least twenty-five feet long. It was peering at us through enormous blue-green eyes.

Eight tentacles were set in the monster's

An astonishing and horrific sight.

head. They were twice as long as its body length and each one was covered in scores of enormous suckers. Its mouth looked just like a giant parrot's beak and its tongue was lined with several rows of sharp teeth.

The whole creature must have weighed more than fifty thousand pounds, and its color changed with incredible speed from gray to reddish brown.

We felt quite safe inside the *Nautilus*. I took up my sketch book and started to draw the creature. Soon, other giant squids joined it.

Just then the *Nautilus* came to a sudden stop. Captain Nemo appeared a moment later. "Nothing to worry about," he said. "I think one of the creatures must have got trapped in the propellers."

"What are you going to do?" I asked.

"We shall surface and drive the creatures away," he replied.

We followed the captain and twelve of his crew up to the main hatch. Most of the crew were carrying axes.

Captain Nemo gave orders for the ship to surface. Then the hatch was opened.

Instantly a huge tentacle slid down through the opening. None of us expected to be attacked like this. The captain grabbed an axe and sliced through the tentacle with one blow.

Now two more tentacles appeared. One grabbed the crewman standing in front of the captain and pulled him upwards with a huge force. The poor man, in the grip of the tentacle, screamed for help. He was gasping and choking. I shall remember his heartrending cry to the end of my days.

The poor fellow was lost. Who could save him from that powerful grip? Nevertheless, Captain Nemo rushed at the squid and hacked off another of its tentacles. He was about to attack again when the squid threw out a blinding jet of black liquid.

When the cloud of black had cleared away, the squid and its victim had disappeared. But other squid kept on attacking us. We joined the crew as they battled to drive the creatures away from the ship.

Ned was about to fire a harpoon into one of the beasts when a tentacle threw him on his back. The huge jaws of the squid opened – he was about to be cut in two. I leapt to his aid, but Captain Nemo was quicker. He plunged his axe into the beast just in time, and saved my friend's life.

He was gasping and choking.

The Giant Squid

We continued to attack the creatures and one by one they swam off. Most had lost several tentacles. Afterwards, I saw Captain Nemo with tears in his eyes. This was the second member of his crew who had been lost since we came aboard. And that poor sailor would never lie in the Coral Cemetery.

His bones would rest in one of the caves of a giant squid forever.

Chapter 21
The Captain's Diary

We didn't see Captain Nemo for several days after the drama of the giant squid. Once more he was in mourning for the loss of one of his family. Under the circumstances, I thought perhaps he might be more sympathetic to freeing us. I decided to go and see him. He wasn't in his cabin, so I began to hunt the ship for him.

I eventually found him in a small cabin at the back of the ship. It was here, I was to discover, that he kept his diary. It was his writing room. He was surprised to see me and quite annoyed that I had disturbed his peace.

"I want to speak to you, Captain," I said.

"I am working," he replied.

"I insist," I said firmly. "I want to ask you for our liberty."

"I told you once and I will tell you again," he replied, "whoever enters the *Nautilus* can never leave her, except by death."

"That is slavery!" I cried.

"I want to speak to you, Captain."

"Call it whatever you like," he said. "No one leaves the *Nautilus*."

"I don't understand," I said. "You weep for a lost member of your crew, yet you have no thought for our own families, who will be heart-broken at our disappearance. They will never know what happened to us."

"Your families will know what happened to you one day," replied the captain, pointing to a manuscript lying open on his desk. "Here, Pro-fessor, is my diary. It includes all my studies of life beneath the oceans. It also holds the story of my life and this expedition. God willing, it will not perish when I die."

"I shall seal this diary in a small unsinkable container and then the last man alive on the ship will throw it overboard. Eventually someone will pick it up and read it. So your own families will learn of how you lived out your life on the *Nautilus*. Now, if you please, you must leave me to my work."

I reported the conversation to Ned and Conseil.

"Right," said Ned. "We must escape at the very next opportunity."

This time I did agree with him. We studied the maps and decided that the seas off New

York might be the next possibility. But before we could do anything about it, a hurricane blew up.

The storm broke on May 18, just as we were off Long Island. Captain Nemo could very well have taken the *Nautilus* into a dive to avoid the storm, but inexplicably, he didn't.

He tied himself to the platform with a rope so the waves could not wash him away. There he stood, as the ship rolled from side to side and the wind tugged at his hair. Torrential rain followed. And still he stayed on the platform, defying the elements.

The hurricane was blasting the ship with hundred-mile-an-hour winds. Fifty foot waves crashed over him. By ten o'clock that night, the sky was on fire. The heavens were streaked with lightning. Yet the captain just stared back at the storm clouds, as though defying the lightning to attack him. This was madness!

The wind howled in at us from all directions at once. The lightning turned the rain into showers of sparks. It seemed to me that Captain Nemo was seeking his own death that night.

During the storm a gigantic wave hit the *Nautilus* and threw her up into the air, the bow of the ship pointing to the sky. The wave passed

And still he stayed on the platform.

away and she crashed back to the surface again. I was surprised to find myself still alive. I quickly retired to my cabin and clung onto the bed for dear life.

It was not until midnight that I heard the *Nautilus'* tanks being filled and the ship starting to dive. Captain Nemo had finally said good-night to the tempest and we were all returning to the peace of the deep.

Chapter 22
Under Attack!

The hurricane finally blew itself out, but any hopes of escape had vanished. We didn't see land again for several days. One thing was for sure, Captain Nemo had no intention of getting any closer to American shores. The *Nautilus* was now heading east.

We next surfaced on a sunny morning, in sight of the English coast, close to Land's End. We had only just surfaced when we heard a large explosion. I was in the drawing room with the captain at the time, and asked what it was. He ignored me, so I went up onto the platform to join Conseil and Ned.

"It was an artillery shot from that ship in the distance," said Ned, pointing.

I looked out and saw a ship several miles away. "Is she firing at us or something else?" I asked. "What kind of ship is she?"

"A man-of-war, no doubt," said Ned. "She's probably just doing firing practice."

"Let's hope she sinks us by accident, so we can escape," said Conseil.

The ship came closer. Now we could see that she was an English warship with two armor-plated decks and a ram on her forward deck. She was approaching rapidly.

A puff of white smoke appeared from the warship. A moment later there was a noisy splash behind the *Nautilus* as a second shell plunged into the water. That was no firing prac-tice – the shell was aimed at us!

Conseil reminded me of the days before we were imprisoned on the ship. "Remember," he said, "how we thought the *Nautilus* was a giant sea creature. Perhaps that's what they think we are."

But I knew it wasn't so. It was at that moment that my mind began to clear.

What about the night we had been drugged? Had Captain Nemo gone out that night and attacked a ship, whilst we were unconscious?

What about the man we saw buried in the Coral Cemetery? Had he been a victim of a collision caused by the *Nautilus* ramming another ship? I was beginning to think that the answer to those questions was "Yes!"

The truth as I saw it now was that, for

whatever reason, Captain Nemo had been taking his revenge against certain nations. Sinking their ships was one way he achieved that.

The fact that the English warship had fired on us told me something else. Since our capture, the world had also discovered that the *Nautilus* was no giant creature of the deep. It was a very dangerous man-made object that had to be destroyed.

I suddenly realized that instead of meeting friends on that warship, we would be treated, along with the captain and his crew, as dangerous enemies.

The warship was closing in on us and firing more and more shells at us.

"We must signal to them," I said. "Let them know we are not enemies."

Ned took out a white signaling flag that was kept on the platform. He was about to wave it when he was felled to the deck by the blow of an iron fist. It was Captain Nemo.

"You fool!" roared the captain. "Do you want me to nail you to the front of the *Nautilus* before it rams that ship?"

Captain Nemo was a terrible sight. His face had grown pale and his wide-open eyes

The shell was aimed at us!

stared into the distance. He had the look of a true madman.

The warship's shells were now raining down around the *Nautilus*.

"Fire as many shells as you like!" he cried into the wind. "What do I care? It will always be me and my crew, and the *Nautilus* against the world! Prepare to die!"

"Are you going to sink the ship?" I asked anxiously.

"Of course," he cried. "Now go below. Get out of my way!"

He was felled to the deck.

Under Attack!

We went down to the drawing room. The *Nautilus* was making no attempt to hide herself. She was sailing fully on the surface and we could follow the action through the drawing room window.

Captain Nemo had put on speed and was forcing the warship to chase him. The hours passed and later I returned to the platform. The captain was still there. He was stalking around like a wild beast. I tried to talk to him, but he started shouting at me again.

"I am the law now!" he cried. "I am justice! I am the oppressed and the warship is my oppressor. It is through ships like her that I lost all that I loved . . . my wife, my children, my father and mother, and my country. Now be gone with you before I throw you overboard."

I hurried below again and told Conseil and Ned that it was time to escape. It was either escape or risk being drowned by the mad Captain Nemo. We decided to take our chance that night. We hoped the warship would be close enough for us to reach it either in the dinghy, or by swimming.

A little after midday, I went up onto the platform again. Captain Nemo was still there, staring back at the warship. She was drawing

"I am the law now!"

closer all the time. For a long time, I simply stood and watched him. He never took his eyes off his enemy. Oh, what hatred I saw in his eyes!

Late in the afternoon, he gave orders for the crew to prepare for an attack and ordered me below once more. The warship opened fire again. Shells were landing all around us. Suddenly, the *Nautilus* veered around and faced its pursuer. I heard Captain Nemo shout out: "Dive! Dive! Dive! Full power! Dead ahead!"

I realized now that the warship and its crew were to be murdered. And murder it was certainly going to be!

The *Nautilus* dived a few feet under the surface and then raced forward. The ship was traveling at an incredible pace; faster than I had ever seen her go before. I couldn't see her target, but I knew the warship must be dead ahead. I also knew that Captain Nemo and the *Nautilus* were aiming at the soft underbelly of the enemy.

The *Nautilus* was going to sink the ship with her harpoon-like, spiral steel snout.

Chapter 23
Murder and Maelstrom

I only felt a slight shudder as the *Nautilus* completed its kill. The spiral snout cut through the enemy's hull like a knife through butter.

I didn't see the actual ramming but I witnessed the warship's fate from the drawing room window. I saw that she was badly holed, and sinking. Water was pouring into the gaping tear in her hull.

The whole terrible disaster was now played out in front of my eyes. First, the sinking hull passed before me. I could see right into the engine room. The crew in there were already drowned or crushed following the ramming.

Now the main decks came in sight. For a moment I could see hundreds of the crew desperately trying to swim to the surface. Some were clawing their way up the main mast with their last breath. The warship was sinking fast. Soon, no one was left alive as the ship continued its final plunge.

The warship was sinking fast.

I stood there, unable to move. I was struck with horror at what was happening.

Captain Nemo must have retired to his cabin because I heard his voice ordering the steersman of the *Nautilus* to follow the warship down to its watery grave. Down, down and down she went until it reached its final resting place.

A few minutes later, the captain walked into the drawing room. He looked at us in a chilly kind of way. "It was them or us," he said. "That's the law of the sea."

He walked out without another word. I followed him. In the corridor I saw again the painting of the young woman and her two pretty children hanging on the wall. Now I knew for sure. They must have been Captain Nemo's wife and children. Hadn't he said that very afternoon that they had all died? Was it the English who had killed them?

Captain Nemo stood looking at the portrait for a few moments and then stretched his arms towards them. He fell on his knees and burst into deep sobs. I felt sorry for him, despite my horror at his cold-blooded murder of more than two hundred crewmen aboard the English warship.

I saw from the instruments in the drawing room that the *Nautilus* was now racing north at speed. We continued in that direction well below the surface for several days, only coming up occasionally to take on new air supplies. During that time we never saw land.

The further we traveled from English waters, the more the *Nautilus* sailed on the surface. A few days later, Ned spotted a distant shore.

This time he didn't hesitate. "We escape

"We escape tonight!"

tonight!" he announced. "Monsieur, you must be ready at ten o'clock. Conseil and I will free the dinghy and you will join us then."

I knew that we must succeed in our plan. Captain Nemo, the mad murderer of the oceans, would never free us.

As the time approached, Conseil and Ned slipped away to do their job. I took the chance to visit the museum one last time, to see Captain Nemo's amazing collection. Then I prepared myself by getting into my heavy sea clothes and collecting the notes I had made on the voyage.

I crept out of my cabin and tiptoed past the half-open doorway of Captain Nemo's cabin. I heard a small noise – he was in there! He had not yet gone to bed. At every sound he made, I imagined him suddenly appearing and asking what I was doing.

Perhaps he was mad, with a desire to avenge the world for the death of his family. Yet, in some strange way, to me he was still a prince of the oceans; the king of the seas.

The captain began to play his organ; not so much a tuneful sound, but a mournful cry of pain. I tiptoed on. Suddenly the music stopped, and I heard him get up and walk towards the door. It was then that he said the last words I ever heard him speak.

"Enough! Enough!" he cried.

What did he mean? Was he at last showing some regret for his murderous activities of revenge?

He appeared at the door. He must have seen me, but he neither said nor did anything. He walked straight past me and vanished into the depths of the ship. I hurried up the main staircase and reached the platform, where Conseil and Ned were waiting for me.

Ned had already removed some of the bolts on the hatch of the compartment which contained the dinghy.

"A few minutes and we will be free," he whispered.

Suddenly, we heard a commotion. Some of the crew had begun shouting and screaming in panic. Then I heard the most terrifying words a sailor could hear: "*Maelstrom! Maelstrom!*"

I now knew exactly where we were. We were in the freezing Arctic Ocean, somewhere off the west coast of Norway. This was the location of the great whirlpool known by every northern sailor as the *maelstrom*.

How many ships had this terrible whirlpool

"Maelstrom! Maelstrom!"

swallowed? Was the *Nautilus* about to join the countless other ships that had been sucked to their deaths? Even the *Nautilus* could not fight the maelstrom.

Now, I also realized something else. Perhaps we were not here by accident. Perhaps Captain Nemo had brought the *Nautilus* to this place on purpose. Perhaps he had chosen the maelstrom as the place for his and the *Nautilus*'s funeral.

Already the edge of the maelstrom had caught us. The *Nautilus*, powerful as she was, began to slip into an uncontrollable spin. I started to feel sick as we were whirled around. It was too late to undo the last bolts on the dinghy. All our strength was needed to hang on. We held onto the little craft with mounting terror.

The force of the whirlpool was awesome. Its power finally cracked the last of the dinghy's bolts. It flew over the side of the ship and we were dragged off with it. We plummeted into the maelstrom. That was the last thing I remembered, before sinking into unconsciousness.

The next thing I knew, I was waking up with Ned and Conseil in a fisherman's hut on the coast of Norway. How we survived and escaped the maelstrom, I will never know. The fisherman had found us on a beach.

I was so thankful that we were all alive. But what had happened to the *Nautilus* and Captain Nemo, and his crew?

Chapter 24

The Captain's True Identity

Here I must make a confession. Yesterday I had the chance to sneak into Captain Nemo's writing cabin. His diary was open on the desk. I just had time to read some of it.

Most of the diary was filled with scientific entries about what he had found beneath the oceans. But as he had told me, there was a short description of his life. I read it with amazement.

It appeared that Captain Nemo's true name was Prince Dakkar. He had been born a prince in a far off land that was once part of India – a country under English rule at the time, many years ago. He spent his youth in Europe and America, studying at the best universities and accumulating great scientific knowledge.

Prince Dakkar returned to his country, hoping to free his land. He wanted to become a great and kindly ruler. He wanted to give his people a proper education and the chance to live free lives. He had dreams for the happiness of all his people. He married a rich Indian princess and they had two children. How he loved his wife and children!

Then he led an uprising against the English. He and his people fought long and hard. Prince Dakkar risked his life many times fighting alongside the poorest and humblest of his people. He fought in twenty battles and was wounded ten times. Tragically for him, the final battle was lost.

During the uprising his wife and children, and his mother and father, were killed. The English also put a price on the prince's head for his capture.

Prince Dakkar was filled with hatred for what had happened to his family and his country. It was then that he decided to turn his back on civilization and the world. With his most loyal and faithful companions for a crew, he sailed to a deserted island in the Pacific and built the *Nautilus*. No wonder he felt so sad when one of his crewmen died.

It is not surprising either, that from time to time he took his revenge by attacking English and European ships.

I would have liked to have had more time to

Reading his diary

study his diary. Let's hope that one day, as the captain promised, it will be thrown overboard for someone to find.

I still cannot fathom out the true nature of Captain Nemo, or Prince Dakkar as I now know him to be. Was he avenger or philosopher, helper of the poor and needy or greedy for the ocean's bounty? And where was he now?

Perhaps his mighty ship had escaped from the grip of that maelstrom. He might be still alive. Perhaps the *Nautilus* had been badly damaged. Perhaps he had managed to sail his beloved vessel back to that deserted island and repair her. Was he, even at this moment, still lurking beneath the waves, ready to strike once more?

In some strange way, I hope the *Nautilus* did survive. I hope the captain still journeys around the world in his magnificent vessel. And if he did survive the maelstrom, then I have one wish for him when he finally dies. And that is that some kind crewman takes him on a final journey to the Coral Cemetery.

There, he would at last be at peace with himself and the world.

Where was he now?

The End

Alice in Wonderland
By Lewis Carroll

When Alice decides to follow a White Rabbit down a rabbit hole, it is the start of her most extraordinary adventures in the nonsensical world of Wonderland.

There she meets some strange and delightful characters, including the King and Queen of Hearts, the Turtle, the Mad Hatter, the March Hare, the Duchess and the grinning Cheshire Cat.

Lewis Carroll's unforgettable story has enchanted young readers for nearly 150 years. The wonderful characters he created still live on around the world, in the dreams and imaginations of children today.

Around the World in 80 Days

By Jules Verne

In 1872 the London gentleman Phileas Fogg makes a £20,000 bet that he can travel around the world in eighty days . . . a nineteenth century challenge as tough as any twenty-first century space mission.

With his loyal servant Passepartout, Mr. Fogg sets off on an astounding race against time; crossing wild oceans by steamship and dangerous continents by railroad, elephant, and even a snow sled! Yet, unknown to Phileas Fogg, the biggest threat to his winning the bet is a Scotland Yard detective called Fix who believes Mr. Fogg is a notorious bank robber.

Phileas Fogg's global race – and Fix's manhunt – is on!

The Call of the Wild

By Jack London

When the pale moon rises over the Klondike
River and the night wolves run, you can still
hear the lonely howl of Buck, the most
famous ghost dog of them all. Generations
of readers have thrilled to the adventures of
big-hearted Buck. Kidnapped, cruelly beaten
and starved, he becomes a legend when he is
shipped to the snowy northlands to work as
a sled dog on the goldfields.

Buck's companions have become almost as
famous. There's Spitz, the dog that Buck
must fight for the leadership of the pack,
the one-eyed Sol-leks, the tragic Curly,
Dave, Joe, Pike, Dub and Dolly. And
there's John Thornton, the man who Buck
comes to love like no other master.

Yet, Buck knows that one day he must leave
the human world, for his ancestors are telling
him to answer the call of the wild.

Lorna Doone

By R.D. Blackmore

Lorna Doone is a romantic adventure that has thrilled generations of young readers. This famous tale of seventeenth century England is set on Exmoor, a wild and lawless land terrorised by the dreaded Doones.

At the heart of the story are John Ridd, a brave young farmer, sworn to avenge his father's murder by the Doones and Carver Doone, a brutal, aristocratic outlaw and killer. Then there is Lorna Doone — the mysterious, dark-eyed beauty who both men would die for.

But who is Lorna Doone? Who were her mother and father? And can John Ridd finally discover her true identity?

Peter Pan

By J.M. Barrie
A new adaptation by
Archie Oliver

"Second to the right and then straight on till
morning . . ."

Every child knows the way to Neverland, the
magical world of Peter Pan and his jealous
fairy friend, Tinker Bell. It's Peter Pan who
mischievously tempts the Darling children,
Wendy, John and Michael, to leave home
and fly away to Neverland. There they meet
the sad Lost Boys, the Indians, the Never
Bird and of course, the dreaded Captain
Hook – and the crocodile determined to
swallow him whole.

Barrie's tale is perhaps the most popular
children's story ever written.

Tales of Robin Hood

A new adaptation by Archie Oliver

When young Robin Hood is tricked into killing one of the King's deer, he is outlawed and sentenced to die by the wicked Sheriff of Nottingham. Robin escapes into the depths of Sherwood Forest and gathers together a band of fellow outlaws. There they begin a fight for justice, stealing from the rich to help the poor.

Leaping from the pages come such legendary heroes as Little John, Will Scarlet, Allan a Dale and Friar Tuck – and their sworn enemies, the Sheriff of Nottingham, Sir Guy of Gisborne and Prince John.

This is the story that has been turned into numerous Hollywood blockbuster movies and television series.

Robinson Crusoe

By Daniel Defoe

Sixteen-year-old Robinson Crusoe lives to
regret the day he ignored his father's advice
and ran away to sea. Captured by pirates,
young Robinson is shipwrecked
and marooned alone on a deserted
tropical island.

After surviving on his own for many years,
he is shocked to discover a mysterious
footprint on the beach! Perhaps he is not
alone after all . . .

Daniel Defoe's famous story about
Robinson Crusoe, Man Friday and the battle
to outwit bloodthirsty visitors to the island
has captivated young readers for
almost 300 years.

The Secret Garden

By Frances Hodgson Burnett

Mary Lennox is an ill-tempered and spoilt little girl. When both her parents die, she is sent to live with her sad uncle in a rambling old manor house. At first, Mary hates the manor house. But in the grounds she discovers a mysterious garden that has been locked up for ten years.

Even more mysteriously, she meets Colin, a sickly boy who has been hidden from the world since the garden was locked. Mary and Colin, and their friend Dickon—an amazing boy who can charm wild animals—help the secret garden to come alive again.

And as the garden blooms once more, its special magic brings happiness to everyone in the unhappy old house.

The Time Machine

By H.G. Wells

In 1890 a Victorian scientist tells his friends
he has built a Time Machine that will take
him far into the future. His friends don't
believe him. But then the man vanishes.
The Time Traveler eventually returns to
tell his friends that he has journeyed
nearly a million years into the future
to the year 802,701.

He reveals how he discovers a new race of
human beings called the Eloi. They seem to
enjoy a perfect life of leisure and enjoyment.
But the nightmarish truth only emerges
when the Time Traveler meets the Morlocks,
a dread underworld race of creatures.

H.G. Wells' vision of the future and the Time
Traveler's extraordinary adventures create a
terrifying masterpiece of science fiction.

Treasure Island

By Robert Louis Stevenson

The one-legged Long John Silver,
treacherous Captain Billy Bones, wicked
Black Dog and the terrifying Blind Pew . . .
they were the cruelest and most frightening
pirates ever to sail the high seas.
They all dreamed of finding Captain Flint's
buried treasure.

But it was young Jim Hawkins, just 14 years
old, who found Flint's map of Treasure
Island. Could he and his friends outwit those
bloodthirsty pirates? And what secrets lay
with Ben Gunn, the wild man of the island?

Robert Louis Stevenson's classic story,
which has thrilled generations of younger
readers, is the most famous pirate
adventure of them all.

The Wizard of Oz

By L.F. Baum

The Wizard of Oz is the famous children's
story that became one of the most popular
movies ever made.

Farm girl Dorothy and her dog Toto are
magically carried away from their Kansas
home to the mysterious Land of Oz. As
millions of children around the world know,
Dorothy must follow the yellow brick road if
she is ever to get home again. On her
journey she meets the Scarecrow who wants
a brain, the Tin Man who wants a heart, the
Cowardly Lion who wants some courage
and, of course, the very mysterious
Wizard of Oz.

This enchanting story delights at every step
along the yellow brick road.

Titles in this series

Anne of Green Gables
Black Beauty
The Call of the Wild
Lorna Doone
The Secret Garden
The Time Machine
Treasure Island
The Wizard of Oz
20,000 Leagues Under the Sea
Alice in Wonderland
Around the World in 80 Days
Heidi
Little Women
Peter Pan
Robin Hood
Robinson Crusoe